BEYOND THE BLUE

This book is dedicated to my beautiful and loving niece Damien ("Mimi") Ferrell

Special Thanks to A.N Mouse for your guidance, advice and encouragement

I'd also like to thank my wonderful mother Katherine Leaver, as you raised me to believe that I could do anything with the right amount of determination.

Contributions by: Jenn Leaver, Autumn Noire, Wahid Nematpoor,

PROLOGUE

Chaos reigned as the burning building began to collapse. There were hundreds of people trapped inside and there was no way they could just jump out a window, since it was a twenty story high rise. Smoke and flames were billowing out every window, and it was so hot, that it was difficult for the fire rescue to get close.

"Look out! It'll block the road! Get back!" someone was shouting.

"Re-direct traffic! It's not safe here!" another called out.

People in the street were running for safety, kids were screaming and crying. Sirens were blaring as more help was called in. Before the road could be cleared, the building crumbled into the street and the crash was devastating. Cars slammed into the rubble, one after another.

Hidden on a rooftop a few buildings over, three demons were amused by the tragedy.

"Would you look at that?" Desmond choked as he laughed. "Those mortals…are so lame! Ahahahaha!"

"That's the funniest….thing….I've ever seen!" Seth agreed, clutching his ribs, as they ached from laughing so much.

"The best part," Luke added, gasping for the breath he needed to speak," is….we…get to do this… every day!"

The three friends continued to laugh until they cried, and they stayed to watch, to see just how successful their session of fun had been.

"How many dead, do you think?" Seth asked when no one had spoken for a while.

"My guess is three hundred and fifty." Desmond estimated. As group leader, it was his pleasure to make the worst of any situation. With average height and brown hair, the green-eyed boy was gifted in destruction and devastation.

"I'll bet it's four hundred." Luke grinned at the thought. "What do you think, Seth?"

"I don't know. I'll say it's around two hundred?" Seth shrugged, not sure what to think.

"Don't go lower, Seth. The whole point of this activity is to wish that more people had died. If you were a true blood like us, you'd understand more." Desmond scolded.

"Well, I'm not. What's so wrong with being a Fallen Angel anyway? It's not like there's much difference really." Seth retorted.

"That's what they all say." Luke and Desmond chorused. Luke was Desmond's lifelong friend and his favourite of the two henchmen. Blonde haired and just downright cool; this kid knew how to get his way, even with Desmond bossing him around. Seth was new to their friendship and he still had a lot to learn. He had secrets from his old life that he dared not share for fear of being abandoned by his new friends. He had no one else in the Trenches to teach him, and he liked the way they were so careless.

"Let's get out of here before the glorified wardens show up. Besides, we have a lot of work to do if we're going to avenge my father's banishment." Des leapt to his feet and the trio teleported themselves to the Demon Trenches, leaving behind the Angels who were too late to catch them in the act.

CHAPTER ONE: DEMON OF A DIFFERENT COLOR

The demon was watching her from behind the trees. Even though he knew that she couldn't see him, he felt safer there. He smiled mischievously as she played in the yard. So young, so innocent. So perfect for his favourite pass time ever. He was about to enter the child and take control of her. The activity was best known as demon possession. The demon's name was Ricky. He was a true-blood demon from the ocean floor itself. Well, at least that's where his kind lived. Hidden deep under the ocean, at the bottom of a trench.

For now, Ricky looked nothing like a demon. His true form was revealed underwater, when he had gills, razor sharp teeth and fins that could propel him through water like a motorboat. But on land, he took on a different form. He looked like a normal teenage boy, but with wolf-like facial features. He had tousled dark brown hair, green eyes and a nose that wasn't exactly human, but took on a more wolf-ish snout. He wore jeans and a black t-shirt with a picture of an eel on it. Not just any eel, but a picture of his fire-breathing Blue Ribbon eel, Fortuna. She followed him wherever he went, even in the Mortal world since she could swim through air just as easily as she swam through water. In this case, she had been left behind. The last thing Ricky needed was her distracting his haunt. After all, Ricky was desperate to get the angels' attention. He wanted to get arrested on purpose so that he could warn them. His brother Desmond was plotting such an evil plan; there was no time to lose. If his previous attempts weren't enough, maybe this would get the angels to arrest him.

Ricky manipulated himself into the young girl and took a minute to get used to her small size. It was at that moment the girl's mother appeared in the doorway of their home.

"Time for dinner!" she called.

Ricky knew that it was now or never. He turned his back and pretended like he hadn't heard, resuming the girl's act of playing in the yard. The mother called again, "Sweetie, it's time for dinner! Come inside please!"

Ricky turned to face the woman and stuck out his tongue, followed by a firm, "No! I want to stay out here and play!"

The girl's mother was clearly getting angry now, as she stepped into the yard to fetch her daughter.

"You're coming inside right now, young lady!" she shouted, advancing quickly.

"But, Mommy, I'm not a young lady! I'm a boy!" Ricky made the girl say.

At this, the mother stopped in her tracks, completely stunned. As the color drained from her face, Ricky took advantage of the moment to start ripping up flowers from the beautifully manicured garden.

"Stop that! Stop that right now!" the mother had reached the point of rage that Ricky found oddly amusing. He couldn't help laughing, and the next thing he did was to set fire to the garden. Realizing that what he'd just done was going to be hard to undo, he paled as it began to reach the dry grass. Panicked, Ricky left the child, not knowing how to fix it.

At that moment, two beings appeared in front of him. They rushed forward and quenched the flames, repairing any damage that had occurred. The flowers were restored as if nothing had happened. These two beings turned toward Ricky, and he got a better look at them from where he hid. The one on the left was slightly taller than the other, with a disapproving look upon her face, and a long strawberry-blonde braid that hung to her waist. She walked with authority of one who had dealt with many disasters before. Her companion seemed a bit different, with short blonde hair which was kept out of her eyes by a headband made of what appeared to be sunlight itself. This was an unusual sight for Ricky, and he continued to stare, taking in the details. Both had a casual style of dress, wearing the most comfortable outfits for their line of work.

They seemed to be looking for him, and Ricky dared not move from his hiding place behind the tree.

"Do you see him Quinn?" the taller angel asked.

Ricky thought that he should just leave, since these two had things under control. As he was about to teleport–

"He's right behind that tree. Hold it right there, demon!" The angel called Quinn shouted.

The other angel pulled out her sword and hit it against a nearby tree. The shock of the blow echoed around Ricky, confusing him. This must be one of the concussion swords he'd heard about from Fallen Angels. What Ricky couldn't understand was how they'd seed him behind the tree. Was it possible that she could see through it?

"You're...angels!" Ricky managed to say, despite having never been captured before. This was also the first time he'd ever seen angels up close.

"And you're in big trouble. Don't you realize that Mortals aren't supposed to be able to behave like that? That's way out of line! Not to mention the fact that it was an under-aged Mortal!" the taller one accused.

"I–just–but..." Ricky stammered. He wanted to explain that all he wanted was a chance to speak, but he was at a loss for words.

"Save it for the Judge." the other girl snapped as she took Ricky's arm roughly. "Grab him, Leila! If I had to guess, I'd say you're no more than a recently graduated demon!"

"Let's go." the one called Leila grabbed his other arm and the two angels sprouted wings and took Ricky to their home island, called Tigris. Tigris was one of four Sky-Lands of the angels' domain. Their island was the west island, the other three being Euphrates Island of the East, Pishon of the North and Gihon of the south. Each island was actually a cluster of smaller islands, easily accessible by flying, unless you were an Amateur. Any amateur angel was required to go through five years of education in the Mortal ways and how to harness and control angel powers. After that, you were tested by going to the Heavenly Falls and jumping off the cliff. If you sprouted wings, you were an angel. If not, you would land in the Pacific Ocean and thus be claimed by the demons, forever known as a fallen angel.

When they reached the island, Ricky looked around eagerly. It was much more amazing than any island he'd ever visited in the Mortal world. To start with, the creatures here were more interesting. They had Pegasi, and griffins among other things. Ricky noticed that the angels didn't fly here. They walked or rode the creatures. There was a large river nearby, he could tell by the sounds of water as it tumbled and skipped over rocks. Also, there was a faint cheering coming from somewhere to his left.

"What's all that cheering?" Ricky couldn't help asking.

"Pegasi training." the second angel snapped. "I was supposed to be there, but I got sent to fetch you instead."

"I'm sorry, I didn't think–

"Yea, you're right. You didn't *think*. You demons are so selfish!" she retorted.

"That's enough, Quinn! Come on!" Leila said. She led the way to the main island, which contained the Parthenon, also known as the Judgment Hall.

As soon as they entered, Leila cleared her throat, "Almighty One, we have come before you with a demon that was caught breaking the laws of immediate Mortal contact."

"Who is the demon and what is his case?" The Almighty's voice rang out all around them.

"His name is Ricky of the Western Trench. The accused is charged with possessing and controlling an under-aged Mortal, and harassing one adult Mortal." Leila reported confidently. She then walked over to the side of the room, where she and Quinn watched and listened.

"What is your status, Ricky of the Western Trench?" the Almighty now addressed the demon.

"I am a true-blood demon, expert level. Recently graduated, Your Almighty-ness." Ricky replied, with a low bow."

"Are you being impertinent?" The Almighty's voice now boomed with offense.

"Absolutely not, Your Greatness. I am merely co-operating with the basic laws. That is, if our realms go by the same ones…" Ricky cast a nervous look over at Leila and Quinn, who nodded curtly.

"Do you recognize the seriousness of your offense, demon?" The Almighty asked.

"I had my reasons for doing so, Oh Great One. I meant no disrespect to the Mortals. Please–" Ricky bowed again.

"Then *why*? Speak now, or be silenced forever!" The Almighty demanded.

"King of the Skies, I humbly ask your forgiveness; as I needed a way to speak with you. My brother Desmond is planning a great evil to conquer you and your realms!"

Ricky said quickly. He didn't think there was any other way to have approached this situation.

"What is this?" The almighty's voice shook the Parthenon.

"My brother, Desmond," Ricky repeated, "is a true-blood senior legendary whose only wish is to avenge our father's banishment! If we don't get out there and stop him, then all of you—all of *us*, will be his slaves forever! He won't rest until he has every mortal and immortal under his command!" Ricky explained.

"How do you know this?" Leila interrupted from the corner where she stood.

"Yes, excellent question, Warrior. How do you know?" The Almighty sounded curious.

"I was out exploring the ocean floor, outside of the Trench, when I saw my brother and two of his friends enter a sunken ship. I followed them, keeping out of sight. I had my pet with me. We heard them talking about it in his hideout…I left after I heard them because I didn't want them to see me. I thought that if I tried to confront them, that I might never get the chance to warn you. Please! Don't let this evil commence!"

There was silence in the Parthenon. Ricky swallowed. Had he said too much? Would they believe him? If not, what would happen to him? Surely not banishment. The worst they would do–

The Almighty's voice broke into his thoughts,

"We will not do anything of the sort."

"What?" Ricky gave his head a shake, not wanting to believe that they could read his thoughts. It could not be possible…could it?

"We have no plans to banish you, demon. You appear to be telling the truth, which is a trait we angels value. If we are to stop this invasion, we need a plan." The Almighty said. "Ahh, yes. You two Demon Hunters will go with him. Take a Pegasi from the Camp and go down to the coast. See what you can find out. If this plan is true, we need to prepare for battle. Go now and hurry!"

Leila and Quinn accepted the mission with haste. They left the Parthenon at a fast pace, flying across Stepping Stone bridge and through the Keeper's Camp before arriving at the Pegasi Fields.

"Trenton?" Leila called out in a low voice, trying not to startle any Pegasi.

A tall, rather handsome angel came out from a small group of Pegasi. He had blonde hair and he moved through the animals as though he were one of them. Trenton was currently wearing a light blue robe, as he did not leave the archipelago as often as his friends did. He patted a chestnut horse as it moved out of his way.

"Well, hello ladies. Is this a new recruit?" Trenton flashed them a perfect smile, as he noticed they were not alone.

Ricky stepped forward to introduce himself, "My name is Ricky and—

"We need a Pegasus. No time to explain." Quinn interrupted. She looked at the herd surrounding them for a suitable mount.

"If you take one of my Pegasi to the Mortal World, I have no choice but to accompany you. These creatures won't listen to anyone else down there. You know as well as I do." Trenton said. "Especially if she's being ridden. Can't you fly, Reggie?"

"My name is *Ricky*. I'm a demon, and as you know, demons can't fly."

"A demon! How did he get here?" Trenton exclaimed, staring between Ricky and Leila with bewilderment, as anger flashed across his usually calm face.

"We'll explain later!" Leila replied. "But we've got to hurry!"

Trenton hesitated, trying to decide if he should help, then went into the midst of the herd and was soon back, followed by a beautiful cream-colored Pegasus.

"Just give me a minute to grab my things from my place." Trenton jogged over to a small grove of palm trees which looked like a cool place to hang out, and soon returned, armed with a golden whip and spray bottle.

"What's that for?" Ricky asked nervously.

"The spray bottle?" Trenton gave a small laugh, "It's Demon repellent, actually. Don't worry. I won't use it on you…yet. Give me reason to, and I will though. This whip, in case you're wondering, can immobilize any beast with a simple flick of my wrist."

The three angels led Ricky and the Pegasus out to the Cliffs where graduation ceremonies usually took place.

"Alright, demon. Up you get. She's okay." Trenton steadied the Pegasus.

"I told you before, my name is Ricky." Ricky said, baring his wolf-like teeth.

"You're still a demon. Come on." Trenton reasoned, giving Ricky a leg up onto the horse.

Ricky sat on the Pegasus, not sure how to hold on. He'd never ridden anything besides the current of the ocean before.

"Just grab her mane, it won't hurt her." Trenton instructed, showing the boy how to do it. "Yes, that's good. Now grip with your knees and don't kick her. Ok, let's fall!"

Trenton, Leila and Quinn jumped off the side of Tigris Island, with the Pegasus carrying Ricky right behind them. They all whooped and cheered as they sprouted wings and flew alongside Ricky.

"Alright. Where are we going?" Trenton asked.

"To stop my brother from taking over the world." Ricky answered. "It's a long story."

"I don't remember seeing you before. Are you one of us? What I mean to say is, were you trained in the Sky-lands?" Trenton tried to sound curious and polite, rather than disgusted at the fact that Ricky was a demon.

"Sadly, no. My brother Desmond and I are true-blood demons. He's proud of it, but I'd rather get as far away from him as possible." Ricky replied.

Trenton groaned inwardly, knowing that working with a true-blood was not going to be easy. He thought of ways to send the Pegasus on its own–after all, Quinn was going, and she knew how to control the Pegasi–but no. This demon could not harm one of his beloved creatures. He had no choice but to accompany the girls and this demon.

"Alright, tell us where to find your brother!" Quinn shouted over the howling wind.

"He's probably planning on bombing a big city right now! So I can only guess at which one!" Ricky shouted back, trying not to be hit in the face with the horse's mane.

"We need to figure out some way to watch for him." Quinn said to Leila, who put a shield around them to block out the wind so they wouldn't have to keep shouting.

"Perhaps a coastal watch? There are angels already roaming the Mortal World, let's call them in!" Leila suggested.

"What? This is our mission! We don't need–

"Quinn, what other choice do we have?" Leila cut in as they slowed down and landed in the street.

"She's right, Quinn. We need a border patrol to let us know the instant that this demon's brother–

"Do not call me a demon! I have a name, you know!" Ricky interrupted.

"Silence!" Trenton snapped. Turning to Leila, he regained his composure and smiled, "As I was saying, we need to know when to attack."

CHAPTER TWO: DESMOND'S CONSPIRACY

It was graduation day for angels-in-training, which meant that the demons would be expecting some new recruits. This time each year, immortals were to graduate. Demons from their realm (all of which were true-bloods), and angels from the Sky-Lands (better known as Fallen Angels if they landed in the ocean). Fallen Angels would be taken in by senior legendary demons–highly trained, that is–and taught to live as demons. Desmond was a senior legendary demon. He was true-blood of course, and he despised everything that had to do with the Sky-Lands. So when an innocent, young immortal fell into the demon realm, he was there to meet it (under the pretence of being a Professor) along with his two best henchmen, Seth and Luke.

The sunken ship that Desmond was using as a makeshift headquarters had once been a warship called the *San Francisco*. Desmond had been there to see it sink, back in the year 1615 after it had been taken down by pirates. The office-like set up he had established was functional and the more they used it the more alive it seemed. The broken architecture was jarring, but there was a chair that Desmond used, a dark wood, high-backed thing that both of his friends insisted couldn't be comfortable and he insisted it was. He had a desk, not that he used it. It was more for the presentation.
It was Luke and Seth who contributed the other things. Coral and anemones, blues and purples and blacks. Demons could see easily in the darkness of the water, so while bio-luminescent creatures were lovely, they were unneeded here.
It wasn't a traditional base of operations, but it served their purposes and they liked it.
Right now, Desmond actually sat in the aforementioned chair. He was upside down, his legs propped tidily against the back of it, his head hanging down and his eyes closed. Thinking. His hair was dark, and messy from being constantly tousled while he was planning. There was a lot

to do.
And while there was potentially infinite time, he was impatient.
"Des?" Luke sat on the edge of his desk and waved a hand in front of the other man's face. Rather than bat it away, Des opened his eyes and settled into a glare. Luke may have immediately regretted the action, knowing that Desmond hated having his thoughts interrupted.
"They found a new fallen. Seth's with them now. Says it's a girl, though. Don't know if she'll be of any use yet." Luke shrugged, feeling a bit helpless.

Desmond sighed.
"Of course she will. What we need right now is numbers, not skill. I have you and Seth to rely on for that."

The rest were angel fodder for the war. He wasn't concerned with their fates. On the other hand, the better the training, the more angels they could get out of his way. It was a delicate balance of taking out the enemy, and making sure his own fatality rates were high enough that he wouldn't have many people to reward when the war was over.
"So we should bring her here then?" Luke asked.

Desmond sighed again and closed his eyes. "Well, Seth should, shouldn't he, as he's the one with her?" He suggested.

He could hear Luke stammering as he tried to find the right answer. "Uh, yes, exactly. That's what I meant. I'll go tell him to bring her here to meet you."
"You do that." He responded lazily.
While he did that, Desmond pulled himself out of his unflattering position, straightened his hair, and set about finding his most sympathetic expression. First impressions were irreversible, even if you really did have eternity to work with. A few kind words, some promise of guidance, and Desmond would have himself another soldier. Nothing could be easier. If only his pet were here to make him feel more like a demon with authority.

Just as Luke left the room, the twelve-foot long eel, a European Conger slithered in.

"There you are, Ori. Where were you? Hunting, I suppose." Desmond said. Ori had been Desmond's best companion since, well, forever. His real name was Orion, but Des hardly ever called him that.

The eel slithered his way over to Desmond, who stroked him in greeting, before coiling around a pillar just behind Desmond's chair. From this position, Des could pet him, or the eel could merely observe.

"We have returned, Professor." Luke appeared in the doorway with Seth. He signalled the girl behind him to wait.

Des checked to be sure that Orion had settled, before allowing his friends to enter. Between them was a young girl, whose demon transformation was still taking place. She must have been beautiful, Des presumed, as her long hair was now entangled with seaweed. She was clearly still confused at having fallen. Desmond knew that Seth and Luke had convinced her to accompany them here, so he could recruit her.

"Hello, young blood. What are you called?" Desmond rose out of his chair, swimming over the desk, to get a closer look at this new girl.

The girl's eyes widened and she placed her hands over her mouth. She was afraid to speak, as she must have been afraid to breathe under water when she first came down.

"It's alright. Relax. You're safe here. You cannot drown." Desmond smiled as kindly as he could without laughing at her. He took her hands away from her mouth and held them steadily in his own.

"Please. Tell me your name, or I shall have to give you a new one." he tried again, ignoring the impatience which was madly flooding through him. Young bloods were so ignorant. They didn't understand why they had fallen, they didn't have a clue how it happened. Desmond only knew of one fallen angel who had confided in him regarding the process of failing.

The girl opened her mouth and inhaled. Des watched as she explored the gills which were on her neck. Des released her hands and she ran her fingers over them as she breathed. She swallowed and finally spoke, "Uh, hi."

"That's more like it." Des relaxed too now. "Ok, now that you're ready to talk, let's get down to business. Seth, let's get our guest a comfortable seat. Luke, would you mind closing the door?" Des sat on top of the desk, facing the girl.

"My name is Desmond, but you will call me Professor Desmond. These are my assistants, Seth and Luke." Desmond paused, "You still haven't told me your name."

"I am Iris." the girl replied, relaxing a bit.

"Well, Iris, welcome to the Western Demon Trenches." Desmond said.

Desmond explained to her that she would join the other new recruits and they would start her training in the morning. When he dismissed her, Seth escorted Iris to her new home.

"What do you think, Des?" Luke asked when they were alone.

"I think she'll do." Des smirked maliciously as he resumed his thoughtful position by sitting upside down on his chair. "When Seth gets back, I want to talk to both of you." Des closed his eyes, which meant that he wanted to be left to his thoughts. He couldn't hear anything from Luke, other than the swirling sound of water, which could only mean that other boy had decided to wait outside for Seth. This was good. It meant that he could have some peace.

It was only a few minutes, however, when Desmond heard them coming back.

"We're ready, Des." Seth's voice cut into Desmond's thoughts like a hot knife. His eyes snapped open and he groaned.

"You couldn't let me finish my thoughts? I swear you're getting worse at patience, Seth." Des said slowly. He remained in the upside-down position, and closed his eyes again.

Seth made a threatening, growling noise from deep in his throat, "Oh come on, Des, you said–

"I know what I said, Seth!" Des snapped; his eyes still closed. "Luke, if he speaks again, hit him for me. Now listen up. If my brother finds out what we're up to, we're all going to get caught. I know he just graduated, which means he's out there, in the Mortal World. We are going to find him, and imprison him if he knows our plan."

CHAPTER THREE: KEEP YOUR FRIENDS CLOSE...

Meanwhile, Ricky and the three angels were descending upon the Mortal world. A coast watch had been set up, so that if Desmond appeared, they would know.

"But how will you know? I mean, if he shows up?" Ricky asked. He was just beginning to understand the angels, but he wanted to be certain that they weren't just going along with his mission to make a fool of him. He knew angels were supposed to be do-gooders and all that. Ricky just had to believe that they were truly helping him.

"We have the ability to communicate telepathically. So by concentration, our messages will be heard." Quinn answered.

"Wow, cool! We can't do that! Is that the only gift that you guys have?" Ricky pressed for more answers. Only then did Ricky realize that his three companions were probably talking about him through telepathy without him actually knowing it. Perhaps their facial expressions would give them away. Ricky studied each face for any sign. Not being able to read them, he shrugged off the thought, and tried to pay attention to what Trenton was saying.

"No. Besides weapon specialties, we can form shield and force fields, or communicate with animals. We sometimes can control the elements." Trenton explained.

"Some of us have other gifts too," Quinn said.

"Such as?" Ricky inquired.

"Well, for example, Quinn has the ability to see through solid objects. The objects are there, they just appear transparent at will." Leila supplied.

Quinn gave a half shrug, as if it were nothing special. "Yeah, I've always been able to do that, I just don't unless I have to."

"Yeah, not since you–

"Don't you dare bring that up!" Quinn warned, not wanting to discuss the time she cheated on her theory exams because she could see the answers the professor thought he'd hidden from prying eyes.

"Do you go on these missions very often?" Ricky changed the subject as he dismounted the Pegasus.

Trenton seemed to focus on the Pegasus for a minute, so Leila fielded the question, "Quinn and I go out for seriously dangerous missions like natural disasters or in this case, takeover attempts. We're both senior legendary, so we're used to it."

Ricky nodded to show he understood, but turned to Trenton, "You don't seem like the questing type. I mean, you work better with the animals…right?"

It was Trenton's turn to nod, "Yes, I prefer it, because it's helpful to those who need to use the creatures or even the Demi-creatures."

Uh, you guys have Demi-Friendlies?" Ricky knew that any creature who roamed the Mortal world that was slightly related to the more mythical creatures of the immortal world was known as Demi-creatures. They were then classified as Friendly or Beast, depending on which realm they derived from. And if they lived in the Mortal world, they were Demi-Friendlies or Demi-beasts.

"If you guys have any sort of educational classes in those Demon Trenches of yours, you'd know that." Trenton said irritably.

"I uh, never really excelled in that class…I only paid attention to the Beasts and Demi-Beasts unit." Ricky said sheepishly. "I only did what I absolutely needed to just to graduate. I thought if I made it, I could spend much more time away from the Trenches. I hate being a demon, even if I am a true-blood. You don't know what it's like down there!"

"Well, we'd understand better if you told us." Leila invited.

Ricky met Leila's gaze, and found that her amber coloured eyes were no longer cold. In fact, they were inquisitive and trusting.

He cleared his throat and gave a non-committal shrug. "It's always dark. Always cold. We can see in the dark though, but…there's not much joy or real fun. I mean, not for me. Fortuna and I usually hang out in the open water."

"Who's Fortuna?" Quinn asked. "Is she a friend?"

"She's my pet, actually. Blue-ribbon eel. She can breathe fire." Ricky grinned, "Actually, the shirt I'm wearing has an image of her on it." he unzipped the hooded sweater he was wearing to show them. The t-shirt itself was black and on the front was an image just as Ricky had described. "She's classified as a Beast, but I say she's not." Ricky insisted. "I'll prove it to you. Let me summon her."

"You're not bringing her around here with a Pegasus in our company. I can't allow that." Trenton put a protective hand on the horse's perfect neck.

"I'm sorry." Ricky hung his head, "I just miss her. I don't know how long this mission will take, and I don't want her to think I've abandoned her."

"We'll see her soon. For now, we need to make our way to the coast." Leila set off down the street.

"Why aren't we flying?" Ricky asked, jogging to keep up.

"We don't really need to. And the Pegasus needs a break." Trenton explained, jerking his head in the creature's direction.

"It'll take us forever to reach the coast at this rate." Ricky sounded desperate. He knew that it was only a matter of time before Desmond discovered what he was up to, and might come after him. Ricky realized that it was probably what the angels expected, and therefore were going to wait and see if it would actually work. He thought about this some more, and in doing so, got distracted and walked right into Quinn.

"Oh, I'm sorry. Why did we stop?" Ricky moved away from Quinn, trying to hide his embarrassment.

"We're listening to an update from the coast patrol. It's easier to hear if we stop and listen. Shh!" Quinn said all this very quickly, before closing her eyes.

Ricky waited nervously, feeling left out. He began to pace, thinking of his own fate. If they failed the mission, Ricky would be outcast. If they succeeded, then Ricky would be a legend, known for making a difference. Before he had a chance to ponder this even further, Trenton called to him,

"Come on, Ricky. We've got to get going. Where's your eel? Perhaps she can spy for us."

Ricky's eyes lit up at the idea, "Yeah! Great!..But…I can't exactly talk to her…"

"Don't worry, I might be able to." Quinn said.

"There's no way! We never learned to communicate with Beasts!" Leila exclaimed.

"How different are they, Leila? Really, as long as she doesn't try anything, if I can get through to her, we might have a chance."

CHAPTER FOUR: ...AND YOUR ENEMIES CLOSER

"We need to find your brother, and we're not sure where to look first. Any ideas?" Trenton was speaking to Ricky, like an equal now. There were no more signs of hostility.

Ricky smiled, glad to be of some use, "Oh, yeah. He's got a ship right off the coast of Peru. I can get Fortuna to see if he's still there."

"Peru? Why there?" Leila asked.

"I don't know. When I graduated, I happened to follow him and his two henchmen there. They seem to stay there for hours on end, doing who knows what." Ricky replied.

"Then we'll have to do that. Summon your eel, and I'll take the Pegasus to a safe distance. She's never seen a Beast and I'm not sure how she'll react the first time." Trenton said.

"Ok, we'll keep you posted." Quinn replied.

As they neared the coast, the angels became suddenly very alert. All three of them exchanged confident looks before facing Ricky.

"He's come up." Ricky too, was confident. He smiled a bit, ready for the first full encounter with his brother.

"You say that as if you know for sure." Trenton said suspiciously.

"I can sense his presence. Echolocation." Ricky shrugged as if the power was insignificant. "He's surfaced, and he won't be alone." Ricky replied. He knew they had a chance of talking to Des, but it might not be enough. Ricky pulled put his dagger thoughtfully, turning it over and over in his hand.

"Put it away, Ricky." Leila warned, "We don't want to start the fight. Let him come to us now."

As she said these words, a slithering blue and yellow creature could be seen swimming through the air toward them. Quinn reached for her bow, ready to strike, but Ricky grabbed her wrist, "No! Don't! That's Fortuna!"

Quinn pulled out of Ricky's grip and strung an arrow on her bow, "If she hurts us, you're dead, Demon." she aimed at the eel, and Ricky ran toward his pet, "Don't hurt them! They're ok, Lucky! Please!"

Trenton had his whip in hand, and Leila's hand was on the hilt of her sword.

"Tell her to behave and we'll put our weapons away!" Quinn warned.

"I'm trying, but she's scared! Please!" Ricky faced the angels, with a mixture of fear and confusion etched on his face. His instinct to defend Fortuna was as strong as his need to stop his brother and right now, Fortuna was more important.

"If she makes one wrong move, its game over." Trenton coiled his whip. Quinn relaxed her arrow and Leila loosened her grip on her sword, but didn't let go completely.

"That's better. Please, Lucky, they're friends." Ricky stroked his pet, comfortingly.

"Why do you call her Lucky if her name is Fortuna?" Trenton asked.

"The name *Fortuna* means lucky, so I just call her that sometimes." Ricky replied. The eel was a fairly timid beast, the angels could see that now. Perhaps Ricky's influence affected her. She sort of hovered next to Ricky, and he didn't take his hand off her.

Fortuna snaked around so that she was facing the coast, and Ricky turned to see what had caught her attention. Trenton, Leila and Quinn stepped forward to join them, and together the group stared at the approaching figures.

"There are four of them?" Trenton asked. "I thought you only said he would have two demon accomplices."

"That's what I thought. I don't recognize the female." Ricky replied, pulling out his dagger.

"We'll soon find out who she is." Trenton said, before turning to the Pegasus. When it took off for the skies, Ricky realized that Trenton had sent it to safety. He stood his ground as they were evenly matched with their quarry.

"Well, I'm glad I found you, little brother, but who are your friends? Don't tell me. They're from the other Trenches?" Desmond raised an eyebrow.

"Ha! Nice try, but you're wrong!" Ricky retorted.

"Uh, boss?" Seth was staring at Leila and he didn't seem too happy about it.

"Seth, I told you not to speak unless spoken to. Shut up!" Des snapped.

"Maybe you should listen to him." Leila glared back at her twin brother. She and Seth seemed to be...was it possible that Seth could still read minds after all this time?

"And who are you?" Des asked.

"Leila, senior legendary angel." Leila announced. "These are my friends, Quinn and Trenton." she nodded in the other angels' direction.

"Well, Ricky, I have to say I'm proud of you. I didn't think you'd last this long before getting caught." Des remarked.

Ricky started to laugh, and he had to use Fortuna as support so he wouldn't fall over. "Lucky, he thinks….he thinks we're in trouble! Ahahahahaha!" Ricky laughed harder.

"What's so funny? Quit laughing!" Luke stepped forward, ready to fight. The angels could see that he was clutching a slingshot in one hand and a small jellyfish in the other. One shot from that and they'd get stung for sure.

"Ricky isn't in any trouble. I think you should have realized by now that we are here to confront you. We have been sent to prevent you from taking over the immortal world." Trenton said confidently. "That's right, demon. We know your plans."

"I don't understand." The female who was behind Desmond spoke for the first time. Desmond turned to hit her, but Ricky was quicker. He jumped on Desmond's back, and put his dagger to his brother's throat. Des roared with fury at having been attacked from behind. Trenton flicked his whip and it coiled around Seth, Luke and the girl, trapping them.

"Hey! Get off me! Let them go! Patrick, I'm going to kill you!" Desmond tried hard to fight Ricky off of him, but he didn't seem to possess the strength. Ricky kept his hold on Des, determination burning in his eyes like fire.

Leila had her sword in hand and Quinn took the demon spray that Trenton tossed to her. Bow and arrows wouldn't work as well in close range, and Quinn hadn't brought her own sword on this journey.

"Where's Ori? Ori, come help me!" Desmond cried out desperately. The slippery grey eel charged out of the water, spewing fire, but Ricky was ready, "Lucky, get him, girl! Go stop him!" he called to Fortuna.

"You're outmatched, here Desmond. We're not giving up until you swear you won't attack the Sky-Lands!" Leila shouted, her sword pointed threateningly at Desmond's throat.

"Fine, I swear you won't attack the Sky-Lands." Des sneered, proud of his own wit.

"But—" the red-headed girl cried out.

"Shut *up*!" Des glared at the girl, then realizing that Leila still had him at sword point, he snarled, "We're leaving. Let them go." Des looked toward Seth and Luke.

Ricky saw the all too familiar look that was exchanged between the angels, and he knew they were deciding what to do. He watched as Trenton retracted his whip, and Leila sheathed her sword, and finally Quinn lowered the demon spray.

"Alright, Fortuna, heel!" Ricky called. Fortuna hissed angrily at Ori before obeying Ricky, who also put his own dagger away.

Desmond scrambled to his feet and snarled again, "You think you've gotten away with this! I'll show you!" He turned to Ricky, "I meant what I said. I'll be back."

CHAPTER FIVE: NOT SO SECRET HIDEOUT

"Come on, get back to the *San Francisco*. All of you, now!" Des pushed Iris and Seth in front of him, with Luke right behind. Des never had to worry about Luke, since he was as faithful and obedient as Orion.

Seth began to protest, "I thought you were going to–

"Just go!" Desmond shouted.

Once inside the safety of the *San Francisco*, Desmond went straight to his chair, but didn't hang upside down. Instead, he sat down as if this were a more formal meeting, his hands automatically reaching for the sextant which lay in front of him. "What in Neptune's name was that?!" he asked.

Iris cowered in the corner, and Seth looked at Luke. Luke stepped forward, but Desmond gave a small smile and held up his hand, "Luke, I wasn't asking you. I was asking Seth."

Seth swallowed hard, not knowing what to say. He cast around for a good explanation. The only one was the truth, but if Desmond found out, then he would be cast out of the group. That would be really bad since Desmond and Luke were the only friends that Seth had at this time, not counting the new recruits that they brought in every so often. He couldn't tell Desmond that Ricky was now making friends with his estranged twin sister. He just couldn't.

"Seth!" Desmond's sharp voice broke into his thoughts.

"Sorry. I don't know what happened." Seth lied. He felt really guilty for lying, but he knew that demons were notorious liars, pathological, even.

Desmond shook his head with a smile, "You're learning well, my young friend. Yet I can still know when you're hiding something from me. I saw that look you gave those three do-gooders. You knew them, didn't you? You knew them before you decided to fall into the Trenches. Who are they? Tell us, so that we may know their weaknesses."

Seth's face fell, he didn't know what to do. He had cared for Leila, and Quinn had been a friend–practically a sister. All that changed on the day he had fallen. He was a demon now, and he needed to act like it.

"Des, it's that girl…the blonde one with the sword. She was my twin sister." Seth admitted. He wondered what would become of them now. Surely Desmond would want to hunt, and possibly even kill them among the others he wanted to destroy.

Des and Luke exchanged looks of surprise.

"Well, well, well." Luke smiled, and was clearly impressed. "That changes things, doesn't it Des?" he asked.

"It sure does, my fine friend. It sure does." Des stroked Ori automatically, and was lost in thought. Now that Des knew there was a connection between Seth and Leila that created serious problems for the angels. It might give the demons an advantage….yes that was it. An angel wouldn't want to attack her own brother, surely. Even if he had fallen. Desmond smiled and laughed at his own ingenuity.

Desmond had been lounging upside-down in his chair for several hours and he still didn't know what to do. Ricky had obtained the best of the best to help him, one of whom was a former sibling of Seth. How he had done it would remain a mystery to him. This made matters difficult and Desmond wanted to be sure that Seth could attack her when the time came. Seth was still rusty when it came to being demonic, and yet Des like having him around. He was useful in angel knowledge…That was it! Angel knowledge!

"SETH!" Desmond's eyes snapped open. He flipped himself out of his chair and headed out of his room, snatching up his trusty wooden staff along the way. Ori snaked after him, eager to be with his master.

"Des, what's wrong?" Luke had been exploring in the next room, waiting to be called upon for conference. This was customary for him, but seeing Des come out and call for Seth...that was new.

"I have an idea, but I need Seth this time. No offense, old friend." Des half-shrugged as he twirled his staff. He hardly used the thing, except when he was "teaching" the new recruits. It was more for show than anything.

"Well, sure. Seth's been catching on quickly. Although he's just headed out to his place. If you hurry, you'll catch him before he reaches the Western Trench." Luke said, trying to be helpful.

"You go get him. I'll be inside." Des said lazily.

"I'm on it!" Luke was gone in a flash, and Des threw an old vase at the opposite wall, where it smashed. He was angry at having wasted time coming up with such a simple solution.

"What was that?" Seth asked, as he appeared in the porthole. Being able to teleport, Luke had simply grabbed Seth and brought him back without explanation.

"Never mind, and just get in here, you lazy Tiburonia." Des ordered, using the scientific name for a jellyfish as an insult.

"Sorry, Professor." Seth realized that Desmond was currently angry and now was not the time to fool around. "What was it you needed?" Seth asked.

"Your knowledge of the Sky-Lands. Demons can't teleport up there, and I doubt Ricky can even do that properly at all." Des began. "I need to know what the angels' weaknesses are!"

Seth began to pace, trying to rack his brain for anything useful. It'd been a while since he needed anything of use from his angel-training days. "I'm thinking, Des, I'm thinking." He said. "The question we must first answer is how does Ricky know what we're up to? You ought to have security around here so that we're not being followed or overheard."

"Nobody knows where this ship is but us!" Des banged his fist on the desk. "I'm sure of it!"

"Oh yeah? Well I'll tell you one thing, boss. Ori isn't the only eel lurking in these waters." Luke chipped in. "There's a blue ribbon out there, lurking in the kelp. Pretty sure it's not wild. Doesn't Ricky have one of those?"

CHAPTER SIX: IMMORTAL FATES

Ricky and the angels were discussing counter-attacks and battle strategies when Quinn suddenly stopped mid-sentence.

"What's up?" Leila asked. She'd seen Quinn get excited about plans before, but she never stopped when in full-flow.

"There's a Beast nearby." Quinn said, standing up to get a better look around. Leila and Trenton followed her gaze, looking for anything unusual.

"I bet it's Fortuna!" Ricky exclaimed, shooting a warning look at Trenton, who had been ready to attack.

"There she is!" Quinn pointed at the eel swimming through the air toward them.

"Lucky! What's the news, girl?" Ricky asked excitedly.

The eel swam over and coiled herself around Ricky, but gazed at Quinn.

"She's been found out. She can't spy for us anymore. If she does…your brother might kill her." Quinn said sadly.
 "Lucky says she only just got out of there."

"You did a great job, my girl. You'd better stay with me now." Ricky stroked his beloved eel.

"That plan's no good then. Now what do we do?" Trenton asked.

"It'll be okay. One of you should rally the Sky-Lands and get ready for a war." Ricky spoke up, eager to help. "Desmond won't rest until he avenges our father's banishment. It's the only way he could have any authority again."

"Your father was banished?!" Trenton, Leila and Quinn exclaimed in shock. None of them knew about this.

"Well, yeah… our father was a true-blood and he was second in command to the Almighty." Ricky explained. "He created all these laws that had loopholes so that demons could get away with a lot more than they do now. When Father was banished after the Almighty was onto him, the laws were rewritten to ensure no loopholes. Things have been different in the last three hundred years, and Desmond vowed to avenge him since. Desmond was promoted to Professor upon graduation, and he's been abusing that authority to train newly Fallen Angels for war, instead of teaching the Demon Basics he was supposed to. At least that's what I heard him telling those two sharks he keeps with him."

The angels had been listening to this with interest and their thoughts were lining up.

"And you didn't report this to your superiors because…?" Leila asked.

Ricky merely looked uncomfortable, realizing how he could have done just that. Had he wanted to be a hero so badly that he thought he could run this mission alone?

"We need to–" Trenton and Leila said together.

"We should probably—" Quinn began, and the three exchanged apologetic grins.

"Leila and I think that an all angel alert is needed. We must obtain the assistance of the other three Sky-Lands." Trenton said.

"I was about to suggest that we send messengers to each Sky-Land. Are there any Friendlies around here?" Quinn asked. Quinn worked best with Friendlies, and often knew just how to use them to her advantage.

"That's clever, Quinn. But how do we keep an eye on my brother if Fortuna can't? If I go, there's a chance I won't come back,"

"Right now we can assume that your brother has gone to get his own reinforcements. We should do the same." Leila suggested.

"But how?" Ricky asked. He wanted proper answers, none of this simplified version of a plan.

"By flying off to warn our allies in the North, East and South regions." Trenton said.

Ricky took out his frustrations on an innocent animal which was scrounging for food. He had kicked it, sending it some ten feet away from them.

"Can you go five minutes without being such a demon?!" Trenton exclaimed, going after the injured creature to comfort it.

"What are you talking about? I haven't done anything wrong!" Ricky snapped defensively.

"That's enough, you two. For the love of the Almighty Angel, can't you just get along for five minutes!" Leila put herself between them. "Please! The Immortal domain is at stake here!"

"I'm innocent!" Ricky protested.

Trenton laughed, "Imagine that! An innocent demon! Hahaha, that'll be the day!"

Ricky glared at Trenton while he snarled and clenched his fists. Leila pulled out her sword and held it up, "Don't make me use this again or you'll wish you had never left the Trenches." she threatened the young demon.

"Ok ok, truce!" Ricky held up both hands in a gesture of surrender.

"Let's figure this out, we don't know how much time we have!"

Trenton glared at Ricky, before exchanging looks with Leila and Quinn. Ricky rolled his eyes and groaned,

"Are you ever going to stop that?! It's really, *really* making me mad. That's not helping me at all." Ricky said.

"Actually, it is helping you. You just don't know it yet." Quinn voiced.

"Oh yeah? How? Prove it! We're wasting time here!" Ricky challenged. He was tired of standing around when they could be doing something useful. He was tired of the angels communicating telepathically and not including him. He was tired of being at the Surface. As much as he hated being a demon, he did secretly enjoy swimming peacefully through the coral reefs every now and then.

"Tell you what. How about I go alert the Sky-Lands myself. I can fly super-fast and I can answer any questions. All I have to do is remain linked with you two and we're all set. In the meantime, lay low and wait for the troops to show up. We'll organize everything when they get here. Ok?" Trenton suggested.

"Since when does a Friendlies Keeper have a plan like that?" Leila raised an eyebrow, clearly impressed.

"Since I joined this mission and all that's happened is my wanting to dispose of this ignorant demon." Trenton retorted.

"Fine, then go. I'll be happier when you're gone." Ricky shot back defensively.

"We'll be waiting right here." Quinn said, trying to bring their attention to the task at hand.

"I'm off. See you soon." Trenton saluted the girls and shot up into the skies.

"Good riddance!" Ricky shouted after him, not even sure if the angel could hear him.

CHAPTER SEVEN: RIVALRY BETWEEN BROTHERS

"What do you have against him anyway?" Quinn asked. They were talking about Trenton, who was currently off rallying the Sky-lands.

"Who, Trenton? Oh. That's just fine. I mean, sure he's awfully intimidating, but I feel with him around I can't even try to be a civilized being." Ricky replied.

"You're a demon. You're not supposed to be civilized. At least not by our standards." Leila pointed out.

"Ouch. You've made your point. Just when I was starting to like you, too." Ricky replied. He turned his attention to his eel, thinking about his fate again. He wanted to like these angels, but it was hard when he didn't really understand them. They had different abilities and they were definitely more experienced. Ricky wondered if Trenton had a chance, and if he could even get enough angels to spare for this. Desmond was tough, but he was also just as experienced. At this rate it was hard to tell. Ricky shook his head a bit, frustrated. "We've just got to beat him!"

"Relax, we'll get him. We should hear from Trenton soon, but we also need to see how many Friendlies we can get to fight with us." Leila said.

****

"What are we going to do now then, Des?" Luke asked. They were in the ship, trying to regroup and come up with a stealthier plan.

"I think Seth should answer that." Desmond suggested, looking over at Seth.

"Me? But I don't know what to do!" Seth exclaimed in a panic.

"Give it a try, Seth; now's your chance." Desmond urged. He wanted Seth to truly understand what it was to be a demon.

Seth swallowed hard and took a few deep breaths, "Well, uh, we should get some scouts...maybe. They could, uh, see if we're being watched?" Seth tried.

"Is that a question or an order?" Desmond asked, with a smirk.

"That's a recommendation for you to decide. I'm quite happy being a henchman thanks." Seth shrugged. He averted his eyes so he didn't have to see the look in Desmond's eyes.

"It's a great idea, Seth." Desmond was almost pleased, "Go send two scouts now, and have them report back here the minute they have any news."

Seth left the room to do as he was told and Luke got up, "What can I do, Professor?"

"I'll need a headcount of our recruits." Desmond said.

"Consider it done!" Luke turned and swam out of the room.

"If you don't have enough, go out and find more!" Desmond called after him, "We need all the help we can get!"

****

Trenton had been to the Sky-Lands of Tigris, Euphrates and Pishon. This left only Gihon Sky-lands. He landed in a camp of some sort, presumably one for the keepers, like the one he sometimes visited at home.
"Hi, there." A male angel strode toward him, a friendly smile on his face. "You're not from around here are you?"
"Hello, friend. My name is Trenton, Pegasi Keeper of the Sky-Land Tigris." Trenton held out a hand in greeting

"Pleased to meet you, Trenton. Welcome to the Gihon Sky-Lands. You can call me Chief, everyone does. I'm in charge of this camp here. Is there anything I can do for you?" the other angel shook Trenton's hand as he said this.
"Certainly, Chief. I would like an audience with the Council member who represents Gihon. Trenton answered.

"Pardon me for being inquisitive, but is it not the responsibility of the Council to inform one another of new business?" Chief inquired.
"Indeed it is, under normal circumstances. However, as the Council is meeting as soon as possible, they asked me to act as messenger. I have a scroll here for them."
Chief showed Trenton to the place where he could talk to the Council, and Trenton knelt down in the presence of the representatives.
"State your name and business." the Council asked.
"I am Trenton of the Sky-Land Tigris. I have been sent here to inform you of a plan to destroy our Almighty." Trenton said, staring at the ground.
The Council was immediately tense, as they made comments to one another in hushed tones. "Do you have proof of this?"

"Here is a scroll, signed by the other three Sky-Land representatives. We require the services of your warriors. We have a demon ally in our custody; he is currently down on the Mortal world with two of the best demon hunters of Tigris. I know this for a fact, since I have been with them thus far."
"Let us see the scroll." Trenton heard the Council say. He held out the scroll without looking up, and felt it being taken from him. There was silence as he heard the note being passed around.
"Rise, Trenton of Tigris." the Council finally spoke. Trenton got to his feet and slowly raised his eyes, but didn't make direct contact with anyone.
"You have no need to be shy. You have done well." The leader said.
"Thank you, Your Lordship." Trenton bowed. "Shall I take a message back to my representatives?"

"That will not be necessary. We will accompany you to Tigris at once. Unless you are returning to your friends below."

"I must return below, yes. However I can assure you that we have angels waiting to escort you inland to the Judgment Hall. That is where we are rallying the troops."

"Very well. You may go. We will leave at once. Your services are commendable." the council said. "Before you go, please tell us who your companions are so that we may commend them as well."

Trenton complied with their request, divulging the names of his friends before leaving at light speed to return to the girls and Ricky.

CHAPTER EIGHT: FLAW AND ORDER

"Trenton's on his way back and he's got news!" Leila exclaimed. Quinn and Ricky got to their feet and stretched. They had been laying low in one of the parks during Trenton's absence, and now Ricky seemed to second guess.

Before he had time to think too much about it, Trenton was there.

"We're all set!" He exclaimed. "I spoke to the Council of the Four Skies. Everyone's meeting at Tigris and we'll go from there. I came back to see if we needed to do anything else down here before joining them." Trenton sounded both exhilarated and out of breath. He took a deep breath and sat down on a rock to rest.

"How did you find us?" Ricky asked incredulously.

Trenton rolled his eyes and scoffed in reply.

"I think we're good here, am I right, Ricky?" Leila asked, hoping to get things back on mutual ground.

Ricky seemed to shrug, "I don't know what Des will do. If he has to other Trenches on his side…but I don't think he will. I've never travelled to them and I don't know how many connections he has."

"We'd better go." Quinn said.

"You've forgotten that I still can't fly, Quinn.' Ricky said,

"The Pegasus you rode down with us will be here in a second." Trenton replied in a clipped tone. He still wasn't one hundred percent certain of Ricky's intentions.

In the meantime, Desmond was once again, upside down in his Captain's chair, fiddling with an old rusted sextant.

"Um, Des?" Luke cleared his throat.

"Hmm?" Des didn't open his eyes, but rather made some sort of non-committal noise to show he was listening.

"We have the recruits gathered back in the Trenches, awaiting your orders." Luke said.

Desmond groaned, knowing that now he had to get up. Being lazy had its advantages, but now was not the time for it.

"Fine. Is Ori here?" Des asked.

"Yes." Luke replied, with a glance upward, noticing that the eel had not been on his usual perch, but rather coiled himself in the rafters above them.

"Okay." Des flipped himself upright, and putting the sextant into his bag, followed Luke out, knowing that Ori would join them.

He assessed the crowd of recruits, most of who had just fallen at the last Ceremony.

"Is this the best we can do?" Des asked.

"These are all who are willing to follow you from home." Seth said.

"There's got to be more! Did you rally the other Trenches?" Des snarled angrily.

"We sent out our scouts, but they haven't returned." Seth replied.

"I asked you to call me when *all* of the recruits were here!" Desmond smacked Seth across the back of his head, causing the boy to bump into Orion, who hissed angrily.

"Easy, Desmond, relax!" Luke pushed between them. "Seth must have thought that the others would be back by now.

Something must have happened. How about Seth and I go check things out and see what's holding them up?"

Desmond glared angrily at Seth, before sighing deeply. "Fine. Go. Be quick about it!"

"Come on, Seth. It's time you stopped being such a rookie!' 'Luke snapped at Seth, who scowled. He thought he'd done a good job. Of course something had to go wrong. It always did when Seth was given a task. When Seth and Luke had teleported away, Des tried to estimate just how many others would be joining his forces to battle the Sky-Lands. He had a brilliant idea. They were going to attack the angels when they least expected it, and they would have the advantage on enemy territory. Desmond smirked as he thought of the greatest piece of information that Seth had ever given him, without realizing just how important it had been. Each of the angels' Sky-Lands hosted a major river. Demons could teleport from one body of water to another, whether it was an ocean, a lake or a river. So Des knew that when he gave the word, they would sneak up on the angels by simply appearing in their sacred river. He laughed out loud, while the other demons gave him blank looks of confusion.

In the meantime, Luke and Seth had appeared in the Northern Trench.

"When are you going to learn?!" Luke shoved Seth away from him, clearly annoyed.

"What did I do *now*?" Seth asked defensively, "Des said he wanted recruits, and I gathered all I could find. The North Demons swore to join!"

"So we will, Brother." said a deep voice.

Seth and Luke turned around to see a ferocious looking demon talking to them, and he was backed by a large group of other demons. Luke could see several Beasts and plenty of weaponry among them.

"I saw how little troops we had, so I forced more to join us. We want to help."

"You're…You're the one they call–" Luke was stammering, trying to get the words out.

"The Raging Typhoon. Yea, I've noticed. Just call me Ty." the demon seemed to swell with pride. "The North goes with you."

"Thanks, uh. Ty." Seth gulped as he cast a nervous glance at Luke, who seemed to have recovered from shock. Seth knew this guy was intimidating but didn't know why. Apparently Luke had learned some things about him, since he knew the demon's name.

"We can't keep Des waiting much longer, we have to leave now." Luke said. He straightened up to try looking a bit more authoritative.

"Are you the one in charge, kid?" Ty asked.

"No, sir. Our boss, Desmond, is leading this operation. I'm his second in command." Luke replied. "Seth here was asked to bring you to him, but we can't wait much longer. We need your team now."

"Well, you have it. Let's move out!" Ty said over his shoulder to his group.

CHAPTER NINE: ORGANIZED CHAOS

Once at the Judgement Hall, the representatives began splitting up their own teams and mixing them up with the others, to make stronger forces. As they were about to head out to the coast of Peru, there was an outcry from the island river.

"They're here! Stand your ground! Archers to the back!"

No one understood how the demons had discovered that their teleportation could connect with the archipelago, but now was not the time to even stop to think about it. They had to protect their land, their kind and the Mortal World itself. With a split second of realization that they were now officially under attack, the angels moved with light speed, grabbing weaponry and surrounding the approaching enemy.

Trenton grabbed a sword from the weapon cache and handed it to Ricky, with a shield. "Use this!" he shouted before grabbing his whip and running ahead. Ricky stood there, stunned speechless. He hadn't expected to even be allowed to fight, nor had he thought that Trenton would ask him to help. He looked around to see where Leila and Quinn had disappeared to. There were so many angels; more than he had thought were in immortal existence. Now that he thought about it, there were very possibly just as many demons that he did not recognize. As he scanned the crowd, dodging the battlers, he saw that Leila was in combat with a pair of fierce looking demons. And hovering over the bridge that connected the main island to the keepers Camp, Quinn was firing arrows at any enemy she saw, and Ty was throwing demons into the river again, hoping they'd be teleported back to the trenches. Ricky smiled sadly, as he knew this tactic was pointless.

"Draw them back to the river!" someone cried.

"We need a team down at the coast! Keep them in the water!" another voice cried.

Ricky spun around just in time to see what could easily have been a hundred angels fling themselves off the island. He turned back just in time to deflect a sword. "Des!" he exclaimed in surprise. Ricky was being challenged by his brother, who had a murderous glare in his piercing blue eyes.

"Time to face reality little brother! Whose side are you on?" Desmond snarled.

"Not yours!" Ricky retorted, as he slashed again, clashing swords with his brother.

"Get him Des!" Seth cried as he ran past, headed for Leila. Leila heard him coming and out of nowhere, an arrow was shot at him. He deflected it easily and laughed, while Quinn said a few choice words.

The battle wore on, angels trying to keep the demons in the water, but Des broke away and went for the main Hall. He thought he could sneak in unseen, but "He's after the Hall! Stop him!" a voice rang out.

Trenton, Leila and Quinn charged after Desmond, but were stopped short by Seth and Luke, "This is our turf now you glorified birds." Luke laughed maliciously.

Out of nowhere, the young demon Iris attacked Leila, who turned and challenged her. "Traitor!"

Iris flushed red and remained silent as she charged Quinn this time.

"You're pathetic!" Quinn exclaimed confidently. But before another word was said, Iris crumpled to the ground, an arrow through her back.

Trenton had taken Quinn's bow, and shot the girl.

"Trent!" Leila cried. "She was one of us!"

"Was. Until she fell!" Trenton scowled, tossing the bow back to Quinn, who caught it with skill.

There was a yell, mingled with a laugh, and the angels turned to see Ricky pinning Desmond to the ground.

"Ricky, no!" Trenton rushed forward and pulled Ricky to his feet. "What are you doing?"

"Get off me! I had him!" Ricky wrenched himself free and lunged at Des again. This time, Leila stepped in and challenged Des to a sword fight, while Trenton threw Ricky aside and deflected a couple of other demons.

Ricky went after Desmond again, despite Trenton's warning. He pushed past Leila, do it was just him and Desmond. The two of them battled their way to the edge of the island. Either one would fall, or both would. Trenton, Leila, Quinn, Ty, Seth and Luke came running over, and stood there, too stunned to do anything. If they tried to interfere, someone would fall to their death. This was war, but the intention was to conquer, not to kill.

"Ricky we don't need to kill him!" Leila called out.

"I don't want to kill him! I want him to let go of the past!" Ricky called back, not taking his eyes off his brother. Desmond deflected Ricky's attack, and threw both swords to the ground. The brothers stood there, panting for air. Ricky dropped his heavy shield, knowing that he had enough protection from the angels if anything. With a quick glance at his new friends, he could tell they were following his every thought.

He also noticed that their eels, Orion and Fortuna were encircling them, also facing off in a challenge. They would not attack unless commanded to do so.

By now, every angel and every demon had noticed the one on one face-off and come to join the onlookers at the shore of the Heavenly Falls.

"Desmond!" Quinn called out, "Let us help you!"

"With what, seraph? What can you do? Bring my father back? He was banished for eternity!"

"We know what you are capable of! We know you're a professor! You could have enjoyed a career with that! Instead you chose to abuse your rights and form an army of revenge!" Leila said.

"Brother…."Ricky said sympathetically. "I only wanted to help you. I didn't know what else to do when I heard that you planned to control the immortal and mortal worlds."

"Shut up, Patrick, you little runt! What do you know?" Desmond bared his teeth angrily.

"I know that you can be a great leader in the Trenches if you care for the creatures we have! Teach them how to hunt for food! Teach them how to create a hideout! Teach them how to control a beast!" Something! Anything!" Ricky pleaded.

Desmond seemed to consider this, and in the second of hesitation, A few angels took the opportunity to rush forward and grab him. He blacked out as one of them hit him with a concussion sword.

CHAPTER TEN: NEW BEGINNINGS

Desmond sat up, rubbing the back of his head. Where was he? He hurt all over as he got to his feet gingerly. The first thing he noticed was that his cherished necklace was now simply a gold chain. The sextant pendant was missing. He snapped the chain off his neck and threw it down in disgust. Great. Then he noticed that his usual attire when roaming the Earth was gone. He was in an unflattering grey t-shirt and grey track pants. He knew he must be in Peru, the landscape was familiar. But where was Ori? Where were Seth and Luke? Des also noticed that his staff was missing. He was unprotected. In the Mortal world.

"Good, you're awake." Trenton was standing in front of Desmond. He'd been assigned to deliver the news.

"What do you want?" Desmond snapped.

Trenton opened a scroll and began to read. "I have come to inform you that you have been officially stripped of your demon status, you are hereby sentenced to a human life, starting at the age of 19 human years. You will choose a surname of your liking, and must never tell any human what you remember, if anything at all. Best of luck.

Trenton finished the letter and took off for his home in the heavens. Desmond barely had a moment to process the news, when he heard a voice.

"Hi there."

Desmond looked around. A young man about his father's age was standing in front of him. He was taller than Des, with a snappy looking business suit and he was carrying one of those flat looking leather boxes with a handle on it. His dark hair was windswept, and he had a moustache. Under the man's bushy eyebrows were sharp blue eyes. Who was he?

"You look lost. Can I help you?" the man was trying to be helpful.

Desmond scowled, "Get out of my way."

The man stepped closer and reached out a hand to Desmond's shoulder, but Des was quicker. He grabbed the man's wrist and twisted it.

"I told you to get out of my way. Leave me alone." He let go of the man and turned away. He took a deep breath and gritted his teeth. "Please." It was the first time he truly meant it in his entire existence.

"Fine. I'll go, but you look like you could use a meal. If you're hungry, meet me down the street at the cafe."

Desmond turned now and faced the man. "You don't even know me...and you want to help me find food?" he didn't understand what this was. He'd heard of generosity, but it was not demon protocol. Nobody offered anything to a demon, unless this strange man *was* a demon.

"Are you a demon?" Desmond asked, daring to risk his own identity.

The strange man pulled a face, "That's a pretty rude question."

Desmond wasn't sorry for being rude, and certainly didn't voice it either. "Well I am." he said. "Which is why I don't understand that if you're human, you can see me?"

The strange man looked confused, and then began to laugh, "You're crazy son, but that offer still stands. Come get some food."

Desmond reluctantly followed the man, who led him down the street at a casual stroll.

Once they reached the cafe, Des looked around, curious now. He'd never entered one of these structures before. There were tables, and people...and they were relaxed. Didn't they realize they were in the presence of a demon?

"So who are you?" Desmond asked the man once he'd ordered food for them.

"My name is Brooks. Adonis Brooks." the man introduced himself.

Desmond suddenly realized that he had once known this man, had even *lived with him.* Adonis was his father. He swallowed, thinking fast. He wasn't so sure that he wanted Adonis to know who he was just yet, if he remembered at all.

"Dad, it's me Desmond. Only now I am going to use the name Desmond Lucas." Desmond decided.

"Desmond Lucas Brooks. If you're going to work for me, we need to share a surname, son." They both recalled that immortals had never had more than one name.

The men talked for a couple of hours, Desmond listening more than talking. He couldn't tell his father what had happened. He vaguely remembered. Something about a lot of people....maybe it had been a dream...he remembered something about water...and light...then nothing.

"I've got to head back to work, Des, but you're welcome to wait at my place if you haven't got anywhere else to go." Adonis offered.

"I'll be fine." Desmond said darkly.

"Take the spare key just in case." Adonis insisted, telling Desmond how to find his apartment.

****

Ricky stood on the cliffs of the Heavenly Falls, his mouth open in a scream that never came.

Trenton came up beside him and spoke in a voice so soft that Ricky had to look up to believe it was Trenton.

"Ricky, we had to. I'm sorry." The older boy said.

Ricky didn't speak. He was trying to process the reality of what he had just done. He had sentenced his own brother to eternal banishment. Just like their father had been. He knew it was wrong, and he felt even more like a demon now than ever.

"I don't deserve to be here. Send me back." He said.

"What are you talking about?" Trenton asked.

"I want to go back to the Trench!" Ricky almost shouted. "I am unworthy to stand on this soil!"

"Not the way we see it." Leila joined them.

"Desmond…" Ricky looked over the cliffs, and Trenton grabbed his arm to keep him from slipping.

"We don't want you to fall. Come on, back this way." Quinn said gently.

Ricky let them lead him silently to where all of the angels had gathered.

"We owe you a debt of gratitude, Patrick of the Western Trench." The Council Leader spoke to him now.

"I banished my own brother." Ricky didn't even look up.

"You saved all of us from his curse." The Council replied, "Which is why we are giving you a choice. You can return to the Trenches with honours, as you are a true blood, or, we are offering to you the rare opportunity of redemption. You will become one of us. An angel."

Ricky looked up now, with wonder in his eyes. This was truly what he had wanted, since forever.

"Can you really do that?" He asked.

"We can, if you wish it. This is a onetime offer. You cannot change your mind once we make our agreement."

"If you'll have me, I'd like to be one of you!" Ricky exclaimed.

"Your reward is redemption. I cast it upon you now. We shall call you Sir Ricky, Guardian of the Skies."

The next thing Ricky knew, he had solid gold wings sprouting from his shoulders, and Fortuna, his good luck charm of an eel, was there. She was now a vibrant blue and gold; completely tame and deemed a Friendly.

CHAPTER ELEVEN: THREE DAYS LATER

Seth was out of breath, beaten and bruised. He had a cut lip, a twisted ankle and a gash in his hand where an arrow had caught him. The battle had ended, and he had narrowly escaped his sister's clutches. Now he turned his back entirely on his past. He was betrayed his former family. He was now and forevermore loyal to the Demons because he had pledged allegiance by fighting for them. He cleaned off the sword he had been using and decided he would now keep it. No, he was stealing it. Smiling a little, he found a way to sort of tie it to his belt for now, until he could make a proper sheath for it. Looking around at the aftermath, he could see several demons had managed to flee, except–

"Luke! No, no, no, no! Lucas!" Seth spotted his pal, lying face down on the ground some twenty feet away. He wasn't moving. As Seth ran over to Luke's side, he noticed the copious amount of blood. He dropped to his knees and turned Luke over. His eyes were closed. Seth shook him hard by the shoulders. "Luke…please…no….please, wake up."

Luke didn't show any signs of responding. Seth was panicking now, almost hyperventilating. He took a deep shuddering breath to try and calm down. Thinking hard, he knew that he would take Luke's body back to the Trenches. There had to be some way of doing so, without drawing attention to them. He could only teleport if he was in water….or was it both in and out of water? Seth wasn't really used to teleporting yet. But he knew he had to now. Luke was dying, if he wasn't already dead. Hoping for the best, Desmond concentrated hard on the *San Francisco*, knowing that Desmond would be there, waiting for their return.

Seth knew he had done it properly when he felt the refreshing tingle of water around him. He opened his eyes and looked around. It was pretty quiet. Leaving Luke floating in the water, Seth swam for the captain's quarters.

"Professor?" he peered into the room. Looking around, he saw that there was no sign of Desmond. Ori wasn't even here, either. Maybe he had not made it back here yet. Where else could he have gone? Seth didn't want to go looking around, in case Desmond came back. So he decided to see what he could do for Luke. The young man was still unconscious when Seth pulled him over to a couch. If it were dry, it would have been quite comfortable looking. However, given the circumstances, in the murky sea, the couch was quite thoroughly soaked and covered in algae and who knew what else. But to a demon, it was considered paradise.

Seth couldn't do anything more for his friend, so he waited. He spent the night at the ship with Luke, which was a huge risk for both of them. Without protection, they were vulnerable to the Beasts which hadn't yet been tamed. He was extra careful to block doors and windows and listened hard in case they had to flee. Seth could have teleported them both to their caves, if he thought of it. But as he waited that first night, he let his thoughts wander to what Leila might be up to. Had she even made it through the fight? Had Quinn? How many, he wondered, had risked their immortal lives and lost them tonight?

By the morning after the battle, Seth woke up to find Luke still unconscious. Desmond hadn't returned either. Seth would've been kicked awake, or else Orion would have been sent to slap him. Seth slipped out for a few minutes to find food, and kept to the shadows, not really wanting to be seen by anyone or anything. He wasn't used to making the plans, or figuring things out on his own. This wasn't going to be easy, but he had to keep trying. It took Seth the better part of the day to get the courage to ask around about Desmond. Not one of the students had heard from Desmond. Three days went by, and Desmond didn't come.

Seth had gone out for one hour each day to ask around, but rumour was that Des had stayed on the mainland.

So with no leader, and no idea of what to do next, Seth thought he had better check on Luke. Luke had been in the ship for three days without any sign of coming around. That's when Seth truly began to panic, even more than usual. He had heard of people being unconscious for days, but this was just downright odd. Luke was tough, strong, mean and agile. He recovered quickly from anything.

That's when Seth realized, with the guiltiest feeling in the pit of his stomach, that Luke may not have been simply unconscious. He then teleported from his little cave in the Western Trenches, right into Luke's room on *the San Francisco*.

He reached out to touch Luke, and found him to be cold. Seth recoiled quickly with a moan of disgust. He wrinkled his nose and moved back. Demons didn't get cold on the ocean floor. It was in their blood. Fallen Angels had to adapt, but it wasn't like this. Luke was stiff, like he'd already been dead for three days. The impact of realization suddenly hit Seth like a ship's anchor hitting the ocean floor.

"I have slept in here…with a dead body…for three…" Seth couldn't even finish his sentence. He shot out of there so fast, that he left an eruption of bubbles in his wake. He would simply abandon ship. Yes, that sounded great. After all, Des was banished; Luke was dead. Seth would have to find someone else to teach him the ways of the Trenches. He thought about the other professors, the ones who actually taught real classes to underage demons. Joining a rookie class was degrading, for sure, but Seth couldn't be unprepared as a demon. Not anymore. His perfect little life as an angel was a thing of the past.

CHAPTER TWELVE: ACCEPTANCE AND DETERMINATION

Things were almost back to normal for the angels. The only difference was that they had a reverse recruit among them. Ricky was demon-born, but was handling the angel life like a pro. He insisted it was due to his time spent in the company of Trenton, Leila and Quinn during the past weeks.

"He'll never truly be one of us." A group of angels were talking in hushed tones, not realizing that he could hear them from where he stood.

"Yea, I know." another angel replied, "I mean, Leila told me that he is special, but he can't read minds like we can.

"We shouldn't gossip about others who can hear what's being said either." Ricky said loudly. The entire group of angels flushed blood red.

"You're right. Sorry." the first angel stepped forward, "How rude of us. Please forgive me."

Ricky looked confused. He hadn't expected this. When he spoke up, he usually got cursed or threatened or even attacked. Slowly, he nodded.

"I forgive you. No harm done." he said with a grin. "The name's Patrick. But you can call me Ricky. Everyone does."

"Ricky, I'm Marty. My friends and I would like the opportunity to know you better." Marty said.

"I'd like that. I don't have very many friends yet, and I'm almost afraid to set foot in the Mortal world right now." Ricky shook hands, and then went on, "You heard about the coast and bank patrol?"

"Yes, we just got off our shift, actually. It's really quiet though."

"What happened to Desmond?" Ricky asked. No one had given him any explanation after he had witnessed his brother get carried off the edge of the archipelago.

"That's not for us to say, Ricky. If you want answers, you might want to speak to the Four Skies on this one." Marty said uncomfortably. Ricky could tell that Marty wanted to say what had happened, and yet they had a moment's understanding that it would be better if Ricky heard it from the authority.

"Come with me?" Ricky invited.

"Wish I could, mate, but I have to get back to the campgrounds. I'm in charge over there, and my students can't be kept waiting." Marty declined.

"Oh, you mean longer than they already have?" Ricky retorted. That was the demon in him, he knew. It would have to stop if he wanted to live here.

"You're a smart mouth, aren't you?" Marty actually smiled, "You got me. Break time's over."

Ricky laughed with him and they parted ways. Marty headed back to camp and Ricky toward the Judgement Hall. He heard a whinny from overhead and looked up. He saw the Pegasus he had ridden on his journey, but it was currently being ridden by Quinn.

"Hey there, Quinn!" Ricky waved and stood back, giving the Pegasus room to land in a cantering gait. It stopped short of Ricky, letting him pet its long nose.

"I saw you over here and came to see what you were up to. I'm just being nosy." Quinn jumped down.

"No worries. I was just hoping to speak with the…correct me if I'm wrong here, the Council of the north skies?" Ricky tried.

Quinn laughed, "*Four* Skies. It's called The Council of the Four Skies. I don't think you'll find all four here, since we ended the battle, but our reps should be inside."

"Oh. So how often to the Four Skies meet?" Ricky asked.

"Three or four times a year, unless something comes up." Quinn replied.

"So…they can tell me how my brother is? I just have to know."

Quinn gave Ricky a sad gaze, and Ricky knew she was reading his mind. He let her in, and waited for her reply.

"I wish I had a sibling sometimes. Leila comes close, but…never mind. Go on in, and be extra polite. Or did you want me to go with you?"

"Please." Ricky relaxed. He was glad that Quinn had been flying around and spotted him.

"Stay here, girl. I'll be right back." Quinn patted the creature and led the way.

"Who is there?" the representatives were in a meeting, but they addressed the two visitors nevertheless.

"Quinn, senior legendary; is accompanying Ricky, honorary recruit." Quinn bowed and Ricky immediately followed suit at the mention of his name.

"Ah, yes, our newcomer. Come closer."

Ricky stepped forward. "Your Honours. I have a simple request to ask of you, if I may."

"You swore your allegiance to us, which means that you cannot go back to the Trenches." The Council said firmly.

"I am aware of our contracted agreement, Majesty. That, I am happy to report, is not an issue."

"Then speak."

"I wonder if you could please be so kind as to inform me of the fate of my now estranged brother." Ricky chose his words as carefully as he knew how.

"Are you referring to the demon who led the attack on this archipelago?" The council rep leader asked.

"Yes, I am." Ricky replied, nodding.

"Desmond has been exiled to a mortal lifetime on Earth. He takes on the age of a teenage boy, and must learn to live there without any power or authority."

Ricky sighed with relief. Des hadn't been killed. He was safe.

"Since we have now told you this, you must know that he will never be able to come within 50 feet of any immortal. He will suddenly forget what he is doing and go the other way. A memory lapse, so to speak"

Quinn put a hand on Ricky's shoulder, "If that's all, we should let them get back to their meeting." she whispered.

Ricky nodded to sow her that he understood, and he bowed to the council, "Thank you for your time. Have a great day!"

Quinn waited this time, for him to lead the way.

"I'm headed back to the Pegasus camp, would you like to come with me and say hello to Trenton?" Quinn offered as she re-mounted the waiting creature.

"Sure, that would be fun!" Ricky climbed up behind her and they took off.

"Hold on tight to me!" Quinn hollered over the rushing wind. "I'm not so good at putting up shields to block the wind!"

Ricky and Quinn were at the campgrounds in a few seconds, whereas it would have taken fifteen minutes to walk.

"There you are!" Trenton hailed them.

"Sorry, we stopped to help Ricky." Quinn replied as they dismounted.

"Good to see you, young blood." Trenton shook hands with Ricky, "Is everything ok?"

"Well, now I know for sure that it is; thanks." Ricky replied. Trenton was confused for a fraction of a second, then smiled, "Yea, your brother. Hey I was thinking, if you like, I can be your brother."

"You'd do that? I thought you didn't like me so much." Ricky was astounded.

"Aww, come on, I was protective of the girls. I always will be. Relax." Trenton smiled genuinely.

"Well, alright then. Can you teach me to work with the Pegasi, brother?" Ricky asked.

"I thought you'd never ask."

CHAPTER THIRTEEN: LOYALTY

Seth woke up in his cave the morning after he'd fled the ship in fright. He lay there, half scared, half miserable, wondering what to do. Being a newly Fallen, he had been in training all this time, but now he had to do a bit of thinking for himself without a professor. He should probably tell someone about Luke, but who? He didn't know if Luke was on speaking terms with his family, and if not, then they wouldn't care. Perhaps a trip to Luke's home would answer a few questions. With that thought firmly in mind, Seth took the few possessions he wanted with hi m (the sword he'd used in battle, the sextant Desmond had often fiddled with, and the slingshot that Luke had once threatened the angels with.)

He swam to Luke's side of the ocean floor city, and found the cave quite easily.

"Hello?" He poked his head in. "Uh, hello, it's Seth! Anybody home?"

When no answer came, Seth let himself in. He went straight to Luke's bed and what he found there left him speechless.

"All this time...and I thought..."Seth stared at the jellyfish that was sprawled out on the bed. At the sound of Seth's voice it got up and squished over to him. Its tentacles brushed against him, and Seth swatted them aside, not yet immune to the stinging. "I'm not Luke." he said to it.

The jellyfish seemed to sag a little. Seth wanted to cheer it up.

"Hey, now, I can take you to him! Would you like that?"

The jellyfish hurried to the cave entrance, swam back to Seth, circled him and Seth got the idea. He laughed and swam after the thing.

It didn't take long for them to race each other to the *San Francisco,* and when they reached it, Seth put a hand on top of the jellyfish, "Wait a second, there."

The jellyfish treaded water next to Seth, who was surprised that it even listened to him. Luke must have done some extra training to get it this way.

Seth had caught his breath, as he was still in training himself, when it came to speed and agility. "Alright, go find Luke."

The jellyfish, whose name Seth had never known, went ahead of him through a porthole. Seth watched it go over to Luke and start nudging him. When Luke didn't respond, it started feeling Luke's chest with its tentacles. Seth became curious. Did this creature have a gift? Could it possibly be trying to revive Luke? If so, would it work? Seth kept real quiet, watching.

The jellyfish seemed to be swelling with energy. The next thing Seth knew, Luke was gasping and coughing, while trying to get the jellyfish off of him. Seth ran forward excitedly, commanding the jellyfish to "heel" as if it were a dog.

"Luke! You're ok, you're ok!" he cheered.

Luke only groaned and lay his head back down. "I need food, you moron. Go get me some food!"

Seth was just happy that his best friend was ok. He smiled at the fact that Luke had demanded food right away before trying to get up. "I'll leave your...jellyfish thing here then, shall I?" Seth asked, gesturing toward the creature.

"That jellyfish *thing* has a name, rookie, and it's Tibbs. Right, pal? Come here, you." Luke reached out for his pet and Seth turned to leave.

"Where's Des?" Luke asked. Seth froze, and faced Luke, not sure how to break the news.

"He's really dead, then." Luke guessed.

"I couldn't save him." Seth mumbled.

"Not if they took him off the edge of that place." Luke replied weakly. "Go get me food."

Seth was more than happy to leave Luke with his pet while he went off to get food. A nice kelp salad should be good...or maybe just a kelp smoothie...yes. Perfect for a recovering patient. Seth hurried to the nearest supply of kelp and set to work on his task, taking care to make it the best smoothie he'd ever made. He wanted Luke to get better so that they could continue doing whatever it was that Luke would plan for them. Luke would have a plan right? Seth thought about this as he swam back to Luke with the smoothie, and then waited for Luke to say something. When Luke showed no intentions of doing so, Seth decided that maybe he could sort of clean up a bit, but stay in Luke's sight in case the latter had something on his mind.

"What *are* you doing?" Luke asked, slightly amused, and mostly tired.

"I just thought that I could make this a more comfortable area for you, unless you'd rather I didn't?" Seth inquired.

"Well, you can cut it out because, frankly I don't care." Luke rolled his eyes.

"So then what *can* I do?" Seth was getting bored of waiting.

"You could take Tibbs out for a bit. He likes to explore." Luke wanted rest, and the jellyfish wouldn't understand.

"You mean, like a dog on a leash?" Seth raised an eyebrow.

"Such a *moron!*" Luke groaned. "Tibbs, go with Seth, bud. He'll show you around the place." he told the creature. It seemed to understand because it went over to Seth and nudged him as if to say "*Let's go.*" In fact, Seth knew that was exactly what it had said, because he used to communicate with animals and had sort of forgotten. He chucked to himself and went off to hang out with the jellyfish.

CHAPTER FOURTEEN: TAMING OF THE SHREWD

Desmond had been a Mortal for three whole days now, and he found it downright dull. His father, Adonis, had welcomed him with open arms. There was food, and shelter, and even a job. Desmond hadn't really worked at all before. Unless you counted the teaching post he had been assigned when he was out of demon. He had thought of it as pleasure, luring innocent (if you could call it that) Fallen Angels into his "academy" as he'd once called his ship. Come to think of it, he missed the *San Francisco* and Luke...Ori and, dare he think it, even Seth.

Desmond was forced to wear a suit and tie (what was the point of wearing the thing when it choked you all the time anyway?), and followed Adonis to the office every day. Once there, he would sit in a small room and listen to people complain about how so-and-so had taken their money, which Desmond learned was a mortal word for currency. After the client was done complaining, Desmond, who was always addressed as Mr. Brooks Jr., was supposed to do a bunch of paperwork. This, he hadn't even bothered with. He figured none of his clients needed the money they were after.

"Where are your files, Junior?" the managing partner of the law firm had stopped by.

"Am I supposed to have files?" Desmond feigned shock and guilt. He hadn't found a new object yet to replace the old feeling he had when addressing a newly Fallen. He had been trying so hard to make this life actually feel normal.

"Don't tell me you haven't recorded any documentation in the three days you've been here, Brooks!" the older man scolded.

Desmond sneered, "My father never said--

"It is mandatory!" the boss cut him off. "We need those files! They help us build the cases for our clients! Do you realize that you just put my whole firm behind by three days, Brooks?" the man was getting warmed up and Desmond was pleased. He liked to see people get riled, and it hadn't happened very much since he'd been a Mortal.

"Whoops. It was my mistake. Sorry boss." Desmond bent his head and turned away so the boss wouldn't see his grin.

"*Sorry* won't get our clients their law suits, son. Of you don't fix this; you and your father are gone. I'm going to talk to him now, as a matter of fact. You have twenty four hours. Move it!"

"Is that an order?" Desmond asked. The door slammed and Desmond could hear the sound of retreating footsteps.

After the boss left his office, Desmond reverted back to his old thinking post and flipped upside down in his office chair. What he didn't realize was that he couldn't do this as a mortal. All the blood rushed to his head and pounded in his ears until Desmond sat up, gasping for air. No more gills. No more thinking upside down. It was time to find a new way to clear his head. Getting up, Desmond looked out his window, watching the weird metal things on wheels moving up and down the street. Adonis said that they were *cars*. They almost looked like snails from here, Desmond observed. Giving his head a shake, Desmond rubbed his temples, unable to focus. He had to do something. Preferably outside; and near the water. That's when it hit him. He could go fishing. Who cares that he was banished. There was no law against an innocent hobby. If they didn't like, it, they would have to compromise. Desmond began to think about getting back to the Trenches. He had to get back. And there had to be a way to take his father with him.

Before he could get too caught up in his thoughts, however, Adonis had stormed into his office and started scolding him in harsh undertones about his reputation and how hard they needed to work if they wanted to keep their jobs.

"Do you *want* to live on the streets, boy?" Adonis asked.

"What difference would that make?" Desmond retorted. "I'll find a way back home, and if you want to come, fine! If not, then leave me alone, for Neptune's sake. You were never there for me growing up; you went and got yourself banished. I only got banished because I tried to avenge you! Now I see that it got me nowhere." Desmond lowered his voice, "If I ever get back to the trenches, I am going to kill Ricky."

Adonis' anger turned into shock. "Ricky? Who in the name of—who is Ricky?"

"Ricky, dad. Your precious little Patrick. Remember him? My annoying little squid of a brother? He's the reason that I got banished. He stopped me. Now he's one of those glorified birds that we hate so much." Desmond was now furiously hissing the words at his father, trying not to give away their previous identity.

Adonis turned and shut the door to the office and locked it. He then made himself comfortable,

"I think it's time you told me the story, son. What did you do, and what do you mean about Ricky being 'one of those glorified birds'?"

Desmond sighed and fell into the chair behind the desk. If he was going to share his life's story, it was certainly going to be a long afternoon.

CHAPTER FIFTEEN: LOST AND FOUND

Seth was led out to a clearing in the ocean floor by the life-saving jellyfish.

"You're not what I expected, you know." Seth said to it. He heard its reply telepathically, and with a saddened heart, knew that it must end. "I'm not supposed to understand you anymore, Tibbs. If I want to be a true demon, I have to close off that connection. I'm sorry."

The jellyfish chose some good words to curse him with, and Seth actually laughed. "Maybe we can keep chatting as long as no one ever finds out."

The clearing they were in was a place Seth had never been to. It was crawling with all sorts of different ocean life. Here, there were eels, goblin sharks, sting rays, and even other jellyfish.

"What is this place?" Seth was itching to explore, but at the same time, he wanted to get out of there fast!

The jellyfish made its way over to a particular grey eel. Twelve foot long and moping, Ori was skimming the ocean floor in no hurry to go anywhere.

"Orion!" Seth exclaimed with joy.

The eel whipped around so fast, that other creatures scattered. Ori saw Seth and sped toward him.

"Whoa! Please don't hurt me!" Seth froze, and shielded his face with his arms. Like that would do him any good. He should have hidden behind a rock or something. Nevertheless, Ori wrapped himself around Seth and emitted a hiss so gentle, that it almost sounded like a purring cat.

"You're alive...wait till Luke sees you! We'd better get you to him right away...no offense Ori, but I'm not really good with eels." Seth said, trying to push the eel off of himself.

The eel spat fire at Seth in an offensive way, and uncoiled himself. Seth immediately felt bad and didn't know what to do. The eel contented itself with following the jellyfish, Tibbs, back out of the clearing.

"Great. Here I am with two sea creatures who won't listen to me, even though I can understand them." Seth grumbled.

When they returned to the ship, Luke called out, "Seth, you're back so soon?"

"Yeah, I am! Look who we found!" Seth called back.

There was a cry of surprise from Luke as Ori went to greet him. Luke played with him for a minute before looking at Seth, "He was at the orphan field, wasn't he?"

"Orphan what?" Seth asked.

Luke sighed impatiently. "When a sea creature is abandoned by its partner, it goes to the orphan field. Was that where you found him?"

"It was a clearing just off the Trench, if that what you mean. I guess it's filled with random creatures." Seth explained.

"That's the place." Luke rolled his eyes. "Glad you brought him back though. He needs us."

CHAPTER SIXTEEN: BACK TO BASICS

"So Professor," Ricky wandered over to where Leila was preparing lessons for the new recruits. "Do you happen to have any tips for a successful term? Ricky asked nervously.

"Well, young blood." Leila looked Ricky in the eyes now. "You're only taking a one year crash course since you won't have to worry about Falling at graduation. Basically we are just getting you to go through the motions."

"Yeah well it's so thrilling to know that I don't have to Fall." Ricky laughed.

Leila groaned and sat up, "Ricky, did Seth ever tell you what it was like when...when he fell?"

"He said it was the coldest, most frightening thing he'd ever lived through. Luke was there when it happened, I guess." Ricky replied. "Apparently their meeting was less than formal."

"You're lucky then." Quinn said as she overheard the last bit. She and Trenton had sought them out.

"I guess I can be grateful. Hey guys." Ricky smiled. "Trenton, are we--

"Come on then, brother. Let's hurry," Trenton answered the question before Ricky asked.

"Stop doing that, really." Ricky implored.

The two of them were headed off to exercise the herd of Pegasus on land before letting them fly for the day. They laughed as they headed off and Quinn stayed with Leila.

"Think they'll be ok?" Quinn asked as she sat down beside her friend.

they will be just fine." Leila thought as she watched the boys leave.

Seth had been stalking the sharks all day, and the one in particular that he wanted was beginning to separate from the group.

"Come on, come on." Seth whispered urgently. *I won't hurt you*

"Are you seriously trying telepathy on that shark, Seth? I thought you'd gotten over that angelic concept."

"Well it was worth a shot, Luke." Seth gave up trying for the moment. "Maybe gain its trust that way o something. Maybe I was wrong to try it."

"You're a demon now Seth, its time you really started acting like it. It's time," Luke glared at Seth meaningfully, "that you got some proper training."

"Teach me" Seth demanded.

"Not me. You'll be attending The Western Trench Academy for Recruits." Luke replied. "It'll teach you the basics, which can be boring since you've been down here a while. but you can learn our laws and what sort of careers are available. Things like that are essential to a happy demon life.

"Happy. You're joking." Seth shook his head sadly.

"Yeah I am. Get used to it." Luke shoved Seth before swimming off toward the Trench. "Let's go, rookie."

CHAPTER SEVENTEEN: THE FRIENDLY BEASTS

Halo Island was the most talked about island in all of Tigris. It was too far from the rest of the archipelago for the rookie angels to get to, as there was no bridge leading to it. The only way to get there was by flying. So it was a perfect hangout for angels like Quinn who wanted some peace and quiet. Today however, she had taken Ricky along to show him around.

"This place is so amazing! I wish I had grown up here!" Ricky exclaimed as they rested in the shade of the trees. He was at peace here. There was a lake here, and it served as a watering hole for those creatures that remained on this particular island. Groves of trees offered plenty of shelter.

"It's nice enough, for sure." Quinn replied as a winged leopard cub came over to her. Curling up in her lap, it purred like a domestic kitten.

"Is that your pet?" Ricky asked, watching the little creature. It seemed to know Quinn, or at least, it wasn't afraid of her. Maybe she was talking to it. Ricky could only guess at this.

"No, I wish. These little guys are so used to us being here, that we take care of them until they are strong enough to fly on their own." Quinn explained.

"So do any of you have pets?" Ricky inquired. He hadn't noticed any as of yet, besides the keeper's herds.

"Not normally, but I had one once. That was a long time ago." Quinn seemed to be lost in thought and Ricky waited for her to continue.

"I remember playing along the riverbank. My parents told me not to, since the current pulls you off the island and over the Falls. I had my leopard with me....it was a lot like this one actually...and it fell in..." Quinn's eyes filled with tears and her voice trembled as she went on, "I tried to rescue it, but Leila held me back. Seth went running to get help but it was too late..."

Ricky felt the sadness emanating from Quinn and he wished there were something he could do.

"I'm...so sorry." he said gently. He couldn't imagine how he'd have felt if something like that had happened to his own eel. She had been his lifelong friend and he hoped that nothing would ever change that.

Quinn shook her head and regained her composure. "It was silly of me as I knew better. Anyway, how did you get your eel?"

Ricky was taken aback by the sudden change of topic but he complied.

"Fortuna? Well each family has a sort of emblem and our family has a connection with eels. So then, on my first day in training, I stumbled across her caught in a trap of some sort. She was up by the reef and I had never seen any beast there before. I set her free and she followed me home. I wasn't sure that my father would let me keep her, so I kept her hidden for awhile." Ricky smiled at the memory of smuggling the eel in and out of his caves.

"Did you know she had immortal powers?" Quinn asked, referring to the eel's fire breath.

"Not until I grabbed her tail one day." Ricky laughed. "That was a big mistake. I was sure that it was going to leave a scar, but I healed almost instantly. Demons are fireproof, as you well know."

"I'll say!" Quinn laughed too. "I bet you learned that lesson quick."

"Yeah, we've bonded really well. I'm glad she gets to stay with me" Ricky smiled. "I will never figure out how she came to be on that reef though. Eels are supposed to like the cold and dark. That reef was anything but. We used to go there to hang out after I graduated."

"Now look at you. A redeemed immortal about to graduate with honours." Quinn teased.

"Hey, it's not as easy as you make it sound, Quinn. I've still got a chance to be banished haven't I? That's one thing every immortal doesn't want...or shouldn't want, rather." Ricky faltered and shook his head, giving up on the topic.

They spent the rest of the afternoon there, lounging in the shade, and occasionally being joined by some of the younger creatures who simply wanted attention. Quinn was able to tell him about each of them, patiently. This was one lesson that Ricky would never forget. Quinn was being nice, and Ricky had found a good friend.

CHAPTER EIGHTEEN: POINT OF VIEW

The first day of school was never any fun for anyone. There was a lot to think about. There were new classmates; new courses; new professors, and in some cases, a new location and a new home. Days like today worried Ricky. Bullies. Defenders. Outsiders.

"Not here." Trenton and Ricky had been sitting in silence, and once again, Trenton had been tuned into the Ricky radio show.

Ricky sighed, almost frustrated. "Why am I nervous then." he said.

"It's new, yes. But we have homeschoolers too. Some even make expert. But every expert had their chance to Fall. You're the first exception of course. "

Ricky shrugged at this, knowing his golden wings were a symbol of honour. That was irreplaceable...or wasn't it?"

"Trenton, you mean there's still a chance I could get banished?"

"Watch your step, little brother. It's a fun life here but you have to do your part." Trenton said. "But hey, Leila's going to see to it that you make it through. You've got me to hang out with, and Quinn offered to tutor you on the side. It's going to be fine."

Ricky relaxed and took a deep breath. This was the life he'd always wanted. He had friends. He had a home. He was savouring it.

"Hey, daydreamer, get your head out of the clouds and help me out, will you?" Trenton called.

"Sorry." Ricky gave his head a quick shake before helping Trenton round up the horses for the night. Not that night actually fell in the Sky-lands but it was definitely colder, which meant the horses needed shelter.

Seth swam into the cave that served as training grounds for the Academy, and he took a good look around. These demons were so young. Like, they were actually just kids.

"I'm supposed to be in high school and this is what I get for Falling?" Seth muttered to himself.

"Welcome, have a seat. You must be Seth."

Seth looked up at the professor, who had a list of names in his hand.

"Yeah I am. Where do I sit?" He asked.

"Stupidity won't get you anywhere, kid." the professor scolded.

"Doesn't answer my question." Seth said loudly enough that he was heard.

"Sit there, seaweed." the professor pointed at a table where a kid was bent over his bag.

"Whatever." Seth said. Joining the kid, he sat there awkwardly, not knowing what to say.

"You're a bit old for this class aren't you?" the kid spoke first.

"Shut up." Seth turned away, already dreading the year.

CHAPTER NINETEEN: END OF ETERNITY

Desmond had finally found his mortal calling. It was a thing of beauty, too. Sure it could be a bit nauseating, but it was just like his good old hideout. This "houseboat", as the people here called it, was moored at the docks. It wouldn't have to go anywhere for him to live there. It would be his home, and he would work as the assistant harbourmaster.

"She's all yours you know." his new boss told him. He was a taller guy, went by the name of Gill.

"The boat?" Desmond clarified.

"Yeah, she's going to need some paint, a little tender loving care, and maybe even a new name. Give her a fresh start. Just like you." Gill said.

"Just like me." Desmond muttered as he stared at his new home. "What shall I call you then? Oh, I know. I'll call it *Orion's Cove.*"

Desmond was lost in thought, deep down. Somewhere out there, beyond the blue, was his oldest friend. Presumably, he was with Luke. Luke wouldn't abandon his best friend's eel, surely.

It took Desmond a few days, but he had the ship in pretty good shape to the point where he was satisfied.

"Nice looking home you got there, son."

Desmond turned, shocked that Adonis had even come down to see him.

"What are you doing here?"

"I just came to see if the rumours were true. I have a lot of friends around here, Desmond. Word gets out that you're fixing up the old abandoned houseboat, and suddenly I am a very important man. "

"Yes, let's just make this all about you then." Desmond scoffed and shook his head as he returned to the tedious task of repairing traps.

"Now, son, don't be like that." Adonis came closer.

But it was no use. Desmond clearly didn't want to talk right now, and Adonis didn't want to lose his son a second time. Sighing deeply, he turned and walked away.

CHAPTER TWENTY: BEYOND THE BLUE

A year had passed in the mortal world, and Desmond had fully adjusted. Although he had grown accustomed, he would never forget his past, or his hopes of returning to his life beyond the blue.

Meanwhile, Ricky was celebrating his recent graduation from the basic training that the angel standards required him to take. Trenton, Quinn and Leila had challenged him to an unofficial Pegasi race.

"What's the prize?" Ricky asked.

"There is no prize, genius, let's just go have fun!" Trenton replied.

So, the four of them were in the air with one lap to go. Ricky had become quite the rider, and was a good challenge for Leila, who had never been one to ride much.

"Is that all you got, Professor?" Ricky taunted.

"Eat my clouds, hero!" she retorted and spurred her horse. Ricky laughed and soared after her. Trenton and Quinn had been in the lead so far, but it seemed like there were two separate races going on between them. Ricky could hear the others urging their horses. The finish line was on Halo Island, where they would let the horses rest before returning home for the night. Ricky flashed back to the first time he'd ever been there and hoped they wouldn't have to talk of pets. Somehow, his eel had gone wild and preferred to stay in the lake on Halo Island. Ricky hadn't seen her in months.

"Ricky, look out!" Trenton shouted.

Ricky pulled up too hard and lost control of his Pegasus. It threw him off and he was falling. The Pegasus was crashing on the island, but Ricky was headed for the Earth. He looked wildly around, willing his wings to appear. Before anything else happened,

"I've got you! Hold on!" Leila had grabbed him and pulled him onto her Pegasus.

It wasn't until they landed on Halo Island that Trenton explained his panicked question.

"Fear won't help you. You need to have confidence and trust to use your wings. Lucky for you, Leila decided to become an expert in riding just in time."

Ricky nodded at Leila and she smiled back. The gratitude was not required vocally.

"What happened to you up there?" Quinn asked.

"Lost focus. That's all. Sorry guys." Ricky shrugged apologetically.

"This Pegasus needs immediate care." Trenton had knelt to look at Ricky's mount. "I've got to get her back."

"You want me to go with you?" Leila asked.

"Someone will come for her." Trenton replied and sat down on the ground.

Ricky wandered over to the lake and stared into the water. Somewhere down there, his eel was snubbing him. He longed to see her again, longed to swim. He pulled off his shirt and dove in.

"Ricky!" Quinn and Leila exclaimed in shock.

"Well come on! Cool off, why don't you?" Ricky waved at them, beckoning.

Shrugging at one another, the girls jumped in, fully clothed. Trenton waited until the injured Pegasus had been carried off before joining them. "We haven't done this in a long time." he laughed.

Seth and Luke were finished teaching for the year. It had been a success, Seth being Luke's assistant. There had been many fights between them but Luke always came out on top.

"You keep that *thing* away from me! It freaks me out, man." Luke was saying as they entered the old ship.

"He doesn't want to hurt you, Luke, he's lonesome." Seth grinned.

"I don't care. If he gets a hold of Tibbs, I'm going to kill you. That's a promise." Luke glared at the goblin shark as it circled around the room.

"He's my pet, and I have control of him. You helped me train him, remember?" Seth said

"Then let me help you train it to leave me alone." Luke threw a rock at the shark. He regretted ever having helped Seth catch and train it. The shark scared his students and was always in the way. It had no powers to speak of and it was just downright annoying.

"Leave him alone, or *we* will leave you alone forever." Seth challenged.

"Good. I wish Des were here instead of you." Luke retaliated.

Seth gasped. He thought that Luke had gotten over Desmond. After all it had been a year, hadn't it? They never spoke of him, and so it was naturally assumed...

"Look, Seth. I'm sorry. I didn't mean...I shouldn't have said...you can stay. Your pet is scaring my students and id like it if you had a little more control. That's all."

"Well its summer break now, so we'll get back to training. Sound fair?" Seth compromised.

"Eight hours a day. Not here." Luke advised.

"You've got a deal." Seth called his pet and the pair left Luke to his thoughts. It seemed that no matter what, the past could not be forgotten. Desmond had left behind a story to be shared for many years to come. Those involved would tell it to their children and so on. The question remained: would Desmond ever find a way to cross back? Only time would tell for those who lived beyond the blue.

ABOUT THE AUTHOR

Brianna is a young author who juggles two jobs on top of everything else. She has a variety of hobbies, none of which are as consuming as writing books and discussing said books with her best friend, who is also an avid writer. Loyal to her church and family, Brianna is almost never at home. When she is, however, she has a pet guinea pig to keep her company.

Brianna has been writing since she was very young, eager to create stories with happy endings and new ideas. Many of these stories have never been shared, and many of them are still being made.

Made in the USA
San Bernardino, CA
01 April 2017